MORGAN COUNTY PUBLIC LIBRARY
110 SOUTH JEFFERSON STREET
MARTINSVILLE, IN   46151

W9-CPF-687

J
398.2
MCD

McDermott, Gerald.

Anansi the spider.

ANANSI THE SPIDER

a tale from the Ashanti

adapted and
illustrated by
Gerald McDermott

Henry Holt and Company

New York

Ghana

for my
Mother
and
Father

PROLOGUE

Folklore . . . Mythology . . . A people's legends . . . Traditional stories
. . . as in Africa. Mythology transforms, making the ordinary into the
magical. It brings beauty to the ways of man, giving him dignity and
expressing his joy in life. Folklore prepares man for adult life. It places
him within his culture. With oral traditions, retold through generations,
the social group maintains its continuity, handing down its culture.

This story is from a long-established culture, the Ashanti of West
Africa, in the country of Ghana. Ghana is a green stronghold of dense
rain forests between the ocean and the desert. This home of the
Ashanti people protects their oral traditions. The Ashanti have had a
federation, a highly organized society, for over four hundred years.
Still, today as long ago, the Ashanti are superb artisans. They excel as
makers of fine metal work and as weavers of beautiful silk fabric.
Into this fabric they weave the rich symbols of their art and folklore—
Sun, Moon, Creation, Universe, the Web of the Cosmos, and Anansi,
The Spider.

Anansi is a folk-hero to the Ashanti. This funny fellow is a rogue, a
wise and loveable trickster. He is a shrewd and cunning figure who
triumphs over larger foes. An animal with human qualities, Anansi is a
mischief maker. He tumbles into many troubles. Here is one of his
adventures.

Anansi.
He is "spider"
to the Ashanti people.

In Ashanti land,
people love this story
of Kwaku Anansi.

Time was, Anansi had six sons....

First son was called See Trouble. He had the gift of seeing trouble a long way off.

Second son was Road Builder.

Thirsty son was River Drinker.

Next son was ame Skinner.

Another son was Stone Thrower.

And last of sons was Cushion. He was very soft.

All were good sons of Anansi.

One time Anansi
went a long way
from home.

Far from home.

He got lost.

He fell into trouble.

Back home was son See Trouble
"Father is in danger!" he cried.
He knew it quickly
and he told those other sons.

Road Builder son said, "Follow me!"

Off he went,
making a road.

They went fast,
those six brothers,
gone to help Anansi.

"Where is
father now?"

"Fish has
swallowed him!"
"Anansi is
inside Fish."

River Drinker
took a big drink.

No more river.

Then Game Skinner
helped father Anansi.
He split open Fish.

More trouble came,
right then.

It was Falcon
took Anans
up in the Sky

"Quick now
Stone Thrower

The stone hit Falcon.
Anansi fell
through the sky.

Now Cushion ran
to help father.

Very soft,
Anansi came down.

They were very happy that spider family.

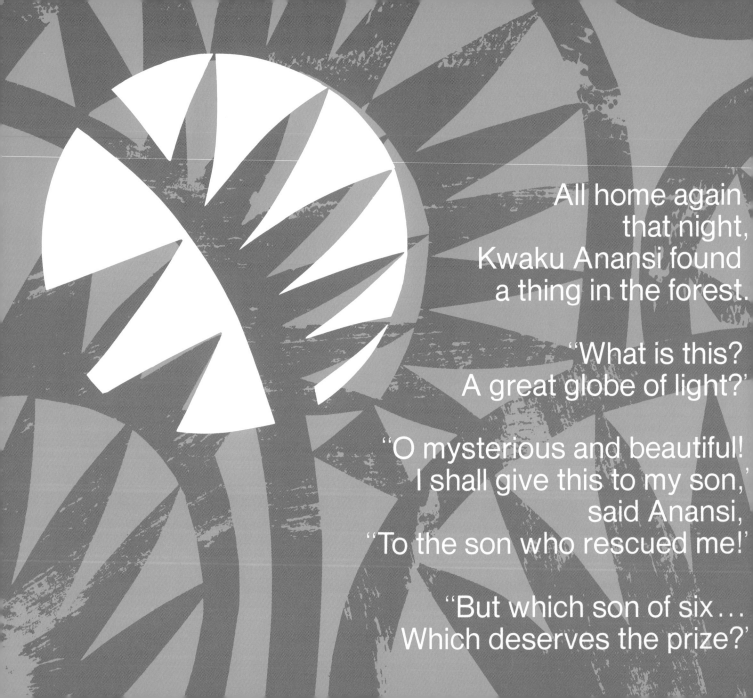

All home again
that night,
Kwaku Anansi found
a thing in the forest.

"What is this?
A great globe of light?'

"O mysterious and beautiful!
I shall give this to my son,'
said Anansi,
"To the son who rescued me!'

"But which son of six ...
Which deserves the prize?'

"Nyame, can you help me?
O Nyame!" called Anansi.

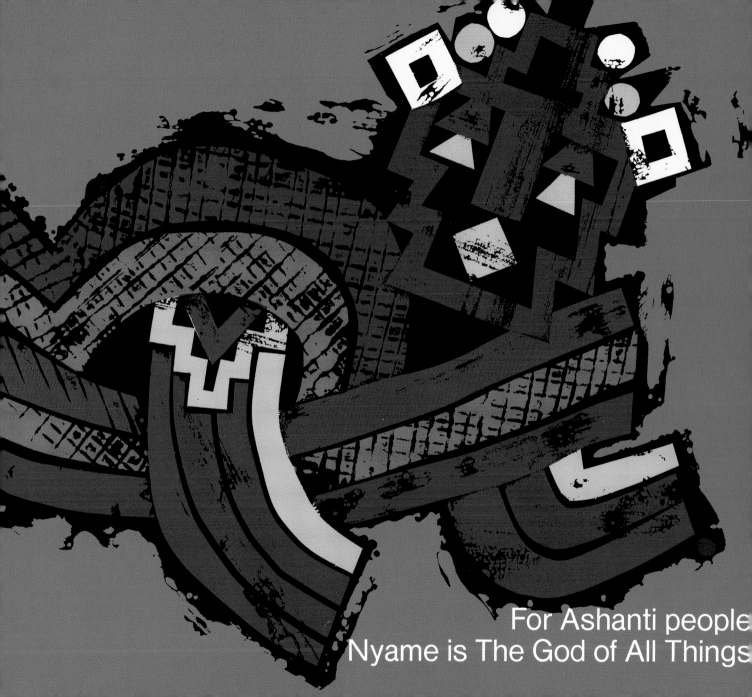

For Ashanti people
Nyame is The God of All Things

Anans
asked this
of Nyame—
"Please hold
the beautifu
globe of ligh
until I know
which son
should have i
for his own

And so they tried
to decide which son
deserved the prize.
They tried,
but they
could not decide.
They argued
all night.

Nyame saw this.

The God of All Things,
He took
the beautiful white light
up into the sky.

He keeps it there
for all to see.
It is still there.
It will always be there.

It is there tonight.

ABOUT THE AUTHOR

Caldecott Medalist Gerald McDermott's illustrated books and animated films have brought him international recognition. He is highly regarded for his culturally diverse works inspired by traditional African and Japanese folktales, hero tales of the Pueblos, and the archetypal mythology of Egypt, Greece, and Rome. It was his fascination with the imagery of African folklore that led him to the story of *Anansi the Spider.*

   Gerald McDermott was born in Detroit, Michigan. He attended Cass Technical High School, where he was awarded a National Scholastic Scholarship to Pratt Institute. Once in New York, he began to produce and direct a series of animated films on mythology in consultation with renowned mythologist Joseph Campbell. These films became the basis for Mr. McDermott's first picture books. Among McDermott's many honors and awards are the Caldecott Medal for *Arrow to the Sun,* a Pueblo myth, and Caldecott honors for *Anansi the Spider: A Tale from the Ashanti* and *Raven: A Trickster Tale from the Pacific Northwest.* In addition, Mr. McDermott is Primary Education Program Director for the Joseph Campbell Foundation.